VASILISSA
THE BEAUTIFUL

VASILISSA THE BEAUTIFUL

A RUSSIAN FOLKTALE ADAPTED BY

Elizabeth Winthrop

ILLUSTRATED BY

Alexander Koshkin

HarperCollins*Publishers*

Library of Congress Cataloging-in-Publication Data
Winthrop, Elizabeth.
  Vasilissa the beautiful : a Russian folktale / adapted by Elizabeth
Winthrop ; illustrated by Alexander Koshkin.
      p.   cm.
  Adaptation of: Vasilisa prekrasnaĩa.
  Summary: A retelling of the old Russian fairy tale in which
beautiful Vasilissa uses the help of her doll to escape from the clutches
of the witch Baba Yaga.
  ISBN 0-06-021662-X. — ISBN 0-06-021663-8 (lib. bdg.)
  ISBN 0-06-443345-5 (pbk.)
  [1. Fairy tales.   2. Folklore—Soviet Union.]   I. Koshkin,
Alexander, ill.   II. Vasilisa prekrasnaĩa.   III. Title.
PZ8.W74Vas   1991   89-26903
398.21—dc20   CIP
[E]   AC

For Nina, who challenges me, sustains me,
and rejoices with me.   —E.W.

For Fillipchik   —A.K.

VASILISSA
THE BEAUTIFUL

any years ago there lived a rich merchant. He and his wife had only one daughter, whose name was Vasilissa. When Vasilissa was still very young, her mother became gravely ill. She called Vasilissa to her bedside.

"Listen well, my child," she said. "I am dying and do not have much time left with you. Take this little doll and carry her with you always. Hide her in your pocket and never show her to anyone. Whenever you are sad or in danger give the doll something to eat and drink. Whisper your troubles to her and she will tell you what to do." The mother kissed her daughter and blessed her, and soon after that, she died.

Vasilissa was very sad. In the midst of her sorrow, she remembered the little doll and took her from her pocket. She set a piece of bread and a cup of milk before the doll and whispered, "My dear mother is dead, and I am so lonely for her."

The doll's eyes began to shine, and suddenly she came alive. She ate a morsel of the bread and took a sip from the cup and said, "Don't weep, little Vasilissa. Shut your eyes and sleep. The morning is wiser than the evening." Vasilissa lay down and slept, and in the morning her sadness had lifted a little.

As time passed, the merchant began to search for a wife who would be a kind stepmother to his little Vasilissa. He decided on a widow with two daughters of her own who were not much older than Vasilissa.

But the stepmother was a cold, cruel woman, who married the merchant for his money. Her two daughters were thin and bony, and since Vasilissa was the most beautiful girl in the village, they were jealous of their new stepsister. They forced her to do all the work around the house while they sat with their arms folded like the ladies at court.

At night, when everyone was fast asleep, Vasilissa would take the doll from her pocket. "Eat a little and drink a little," she would say, "and listen to my story. My stepmother and her daughters wish to drive me out of my own father's house. What shall I do?"

And every night the little doll's eyes would shine, and she would come alive. Once she had eaten and drunk her share, she would whisper words of comfort to Vasilissa until the girl fell asleep.

Years passed, and Vasilissa grew more beautiful. Young men of the village began to ask for her hand in marriage. This enraged the stepmother, who cried, "Never shall the younger be wed before the older ones!" Each time she drove a suitor from the door, she would soothe her fury by beating her stepdaughter. The only joy in Vasilissa's life came from the little doll which she kept safely hidden in her pocket.

There came a time when the merchant had to go on a long journey to a distant land. He bade farewell to his wife and her two daughters, kissed Vasilissa, and gave her his blessing. As soon as he left, his wife sold his house, packed all his goods, and moved the family to another house at the edge of a gloomy forest.

Deep in this forest, as the stepmother well knew, lived an old witch named Baba Yaga. She lived alone in a miserable hut that stood on chicken legs at the edge of a clearing. No one dared go near the hut, for it was rumored that Baba Yaga ate people as one eats chickens. Every day the stepmother sent Vasilissa into the forest to search for flowers and berries, hoping the girl would be devoured by the old witch. But the little doll did not let her go near Baba Yaga's hut, and every day when Vasilissa came safely home, the stepmother hated her even more.

One autumn evening, the stepmother called the three girls to her and gave them each a task. One was to make a piece of lace, the other to knit a pair of stockings, and Vasilissa was to spin a basketful of flax. Then the stepmother put out all the fires in the house and went to bed, leaving only one candle lighted.

After three hours, the elder daughter put out the candle, just as her mother had instructed her to do.

"What shall we do?" she cried in mock alarm. "There is no light in the house."

"One of us will have to fetch fire from Baba Yaga," said the other sister. "She is the only one who lives nearby."

"I don't need light," said the sister who was making lace. "I have enough light from my steel pins."

"And I have enough light from my silver needles," cried the sister who was knitting the stockings. "Vasilissa, you will have to go, for you have no light from your flax."

The sisters pushed Vasilissa out of the house, and locked the door, crying, "You cannot come back until you bring us light."

Vasilissa sat down on the doorstep. From one pocket she took the tiny doll and from the other, the bits she always saved from her own supper. "Eat a little and drink a little and listen to my story. I must go into the dark forest to Baba Yaga's hut to get some fire, and I am terrified that she will eat me. Tell me what to do."

"Do not fear, little Vasilissa," the doll said. "As long as I am with you, no harm shall come to you."

Vasilissa put the doll back into her pocket and entered the forest. Suddenly she heard the beating of hooves, and a man on horseback galloped past her. He was dressed all in white. His horse was milk-white, and its harness was white. Just as he passed her, the night paled into dawn.

Vasilissa went a little farther, and again she heard the beating of a horse's hooves and there came another man on horseback. He was dressed all in red, and the horse under him was blood-red, and its harness was red. Just as he passed her, the sun rose.

Vasilissa walked on until she could find no path through the forest and she had no food to bring her little doll to life. As the light began to fade again, she came to the clearing where Baba Yaga's miserable little hut stood on its chicken legs. The wall around the hut was made of human bones, and the top of the wall was decorated with human skulls. The sight filled Vasilissa with fear.

Suddenly a third horseman came galloping up. He was dressed all in black, and his horse was coal-black, and its harness was black. As he thundered up to the gate of the hut, he disappeared as if the earth had swallowed him up. At that moment, night came and the forest grew dark. The skulls on the wall lit up, and the clearing around the hut was as bright as day.

Suddenly the forest was filled with a terrible noise, and Baba Yaga came flying through the trees. She was riding in a great iron mortar and driving it with a pestle, and as she rode, she swept away her trail with a kitchen broom. She stopped at the gate and cried:

"Little House, Little House,

Turn your back to the forest and your face to me."

The little hut spun around to face her and stopped. Baba Yaga began to sniff, first in one direction and then another. "FOO! FOO! I smell the smell of a human. Show yourself whoever you are!"

Trembling with fear, Vasilissa stepped forward. Bowing low, she said, "It is only me, Vasilissa. My stepmother has sent me to you to fetch some fire."

"I know your stepmother," said the old witch. "If you want my fire, you will have to stay and work for it. If not, I will eat you for my supper." Then she turned to the gate and shouted, "My strong locks, unlock! My stout gate, open!" They obeyed in an instant, and Baba Yaga swooped in. Once Vasilissa had passed through, the gate slammed shut and the locks snapped back into place.

"Bring me all the food from the oven," Baba Yaga shouted, and Vasilissa hurried to obey. There was enough food for three strong men, but Baba Yaga ate it all, leaving only a tiny shred of meat and a crust of bread for Vasilissa.

Then the old witch lay down on the stove. "Tomorrow when I leave," she said, "you must clean the yard, sweep the floors, and cook my supper. Then take a bushel of wheat from my storehouse and pick out of it all the black grains and all the wild peas. If you do not do as I have asked, I will eat you for my supper." Then she turned to the wall and soon began to snore.

Vasilissa went into the corner and took the tiny doll from her pocket. "Eat a little and drink a little and listen to my story," she said. "I am locked in this old witch's hut, and if I do not do all that she has ordered, she will eat me for supper tomorrow. What shall I do?"

The doll ate a bit of the bread and a snippet of the meat and said, "Do not be afraid, Vasilissa. Say your prayers and go to sleep. Remember, the morning is wiser than the evening."

The next morning Vasilissa rose early. When she looked out the window, she saw the white horseman gallop from around the corner of the hut. As he cleared the wall, the night paled into dawn. The old witch whistled for her mortar and pestle, and as she climbed into the mortar, the blood-red horseman galloped from around the corner. He leaped over the wall, and at that very moment, the sun rose. At a command from Baba Yaga, the gate swung open and the old witch rode off, sweeping away the trail with her kitchen broom.

The yard was clean and the floors of the hut had been swept. The little doll was sitting in the storehouse picking the last black grains and wild peas from a bushel of wheat. So Vasilissa rested all day, and when evening came, she laid the table for the old witch's supper and sat looking out the window.

As it had happened before, just as the coal-black horseman came galloping up to the gate and disappeared, night fell. The eyes of the skulls began to shine. Soon the trees began to groan and creak, and Baba Yaga rode up in her huge iron mortar. "Well, have you done all that I ordered?" she asked.

"See for yourself, Baba Yaga," answered Vasilissa.

Baba Yaga went all about the place, sniffing in the corners and tapping with her pestle. Try as she might, she could find nothing to complain of. There was not a weed left in the yard, nor a speck of dust on the floors, nor a single black grain or wild pea in the wheat.

Although the witch was greatly angered, she was forced to act pleased. "You have done well," she said. Then she clapped her hands and shouted, "Ho, my faithful friends, grind my wheat." Immediately, three pairs of hands appeared, seized the wheat, and carried it away.

Vasilissa set the witch's supper on the table, and although there was enough food for four strong men, the old witch ate it, bones and all, leaving only a small morsel for Vasilissa. Then she stretched herself out on the stove and said, "Tomorrow, you must do all that you have done today, and besides these tasks, you must take from the storehouse a half bushel of poppy seeds and clean them one by one." Then she fell asleep.

Vasilissa fed her little doll and crept into a corner to sleep. And once again, the next morning all the tasks were done, and when Baba Yaga returned that evening, she could find nothing to complain of.

She clapped her hands and shouted, "Ho, my faithful friends, press the oil out of my poppy seeds." And as before, three pairs of hands appeared in the air, and carried away the poppy seeds.

Vasilissa set the supper in front of the old witch, and Baba Yaga ate enough for five strong men while Vasilissa waited and watched.

"Why do you stand there as if you were dumb?" the witch snapped angrily.

"I did not speak because I did not dare," answered Vasilissa. "But if you will allow me, Baba Yaga, I wish to ask some questions."

"Remember Vasilissa, if you know too much, you will grow old too soon. What do you wish to ask?"

"When I came to your hut, a white horseman passed me by. Who was he?"

"That was my bright, white day," answered Baba Yaga. "He is a servant of mine. He cannot hurt you. Ask me more."

"Afterward, another rider overtook the first. He was dressed all in red, and his horse was blood-red. Who was he?"

"He too is my servant, the round red sun," answered Baba Yaga. "He cannot hurt you either. Ask me another."

"There was a third rider," said Vasilissa. "He was dressed all in black, and his horse was coal-black. Who was he?"

"My servant, the dark, black night," said the old witch angrily. "He also cannot harm you. Ask me more."

But Vasilissa remembered what the witch had said, and she remained silent.

"Ask me more," roared the old witch. "Ask me about the three pairs of hands that serve me."

"Three questions are enough for me," Vasilissa replied. "I would not wish to grow old too soon."

"It is well you did not ask of the three pairs of hands, for they would have seized you and ground you up for my supper. Now it is my turn. How is it that you have been able to do all the tasks I required of you?"

Vasilissa was so terrified that she almost told the old witch the secret of the little doll. Just in time, she remembered her mother's warning and said, "The blessing of my dead mother helps me in all things."

The witch sprang up from her chair. "Get out of my house this instant!" she shrieked. "No one who bears a blessing should cross my threshold."

Vasilissa ran as fast as she could. Baba Yaga seized one of the skulls with the burning eyes and threw it after her. "Here is the fire you came for," she shouted. "Take it and have the joy of it."

Vasilissa set the skull on the end of a stick and hurried home. All the night long, the skull lit a path through the woods, and toward the evening of the next day, Vasilissa came out of the forest to her stepmother's house.

"Surely they will have found some fire by now," thought Vasilissa, and she threw the skull into the bushes. But the skull called to her, "Do not throw me away, beautiful Vasilissa. Take me to your stepmother."

Vasilissa saw no light through the windows of the house, so she picked up the skull and carried it inside.

For once, the stepmother and her two daughters welcomed Vasilissa with cries of joy, for ever since she had left, they had been unable to make a light burn in the house.

"Perhaps your light will keep," cried the stepmother. She set the skull down in the middle of the room. The skull fixed its steady fiery eyes on the stepmother and her two daughters, and no matter which way they turned they could not escape from its hot glare. By morning, all three had been burned to ashes. Only Vasilissa was spared.

Vasilissa buried the skull in the ground, locked the house, and left. She took refuge with a kind old woman who lived all alone near the town gates where she waited for her father's return.

One day she said to the old woman, "Please, grandmother, buy me some flax to spin into thread. The days are long and my hands need work."

The old woman bought her some flax and Vasilissa set to work. Soon there was enough thread to weave a dozen shirts. When the old woman had gone to sleep, Vasilissa took the tiny doll from her pocket, set some food and drink before her, and said, "Eat a little and drink a little and listen to my story. I have spun beautiful thread, but I have no loom on which to weave it."

"Bring me some wood and an old basket and a few hairs from a horse's mane, and I will arrange everything for you," said the little doll.

When Vasilissa woke the next morning, there stood a loom, perfectly suited for her delicate thread.

All winter long, Vasilissa sat weaving her thread into linen. Then she bleached the linen and gave it to the old woman. "Take it to the market and sell it. The money you receive shall pay for my food and lodging."

The old woman would not hear of it. "No one should wear

this beautiful cloth but the Tsar himself. Tomorrow I shall take it to the palace."

All the next day, the old woman walked up and down in front of the Tsar's palace, refusing to speak to any of his servants. At last, the Tsar himself threw open his window and asked her what she wanted of him.

The old woman showed him the wondrous white cloth. "What will you take for it, old woman?" he asked.

"Nothing, sire," she replied. "I have brought it to you as a gift."

The Tsar thanked her for the fine linen cloth and sent her home in a carriage loaded with riches.

Then he called in the seamstresses to make him some shirts, but not one was skillful enough to work with the fine linen. The Tsar sent for the old woman. "If you know how to spin such thread and weave such fine linen, then you must know how to sew me some shirts from it."

"Oh, Your Majesty," cried the old woman, "it is my adopted daughter who did the work."

"Take it back to her then," said the Tsar, "and ask her to sew me the shirts."

Vasilissa was beside herself with joy when she heard what the Tsar had said. She locked herself in her room and didn't leave it until she had made him a dozen fine shirts. When the old woman presented the Tsar with the shirts, he was so impressed with the fine workmanship that he wanted to meet her immediately.

The moment the Tsar's eyes fell upon Vasilissa, he fell helplessly in love with her.

"Beautiful Vasilissa," he said. "Come and be my wife, and never will I leave your side."

So the Tsar and Vasilissa were married. The wedding feast lasted for three days and three nights, and everyone in the land was invited.

When Vasilissa's father returned from his long journey, he was filled with happiness to find his beautiful Vasilissa married to the Tsar and living in the palace.

As for the little doll—Vasilissa kept her always with her.

About The Tale of
Vasilissa the Beautiful

I was intrigued by the story of Vasilissa the Beautiful the first time I read it. First of all, there are echoes of my favorite fairy tales from childhood, "Cinderella" and "Hansel and Gretel." Second, I was attracted to the visual elements of the story: the magnificent horsemen who drag time along behind them, the skulls that light up at night, and Baba Yaga's miserable hut on chicken legs, to name just a few. And finally, I particularly loved this story because it is a tale peopled by women. From Vasilissa's mother and her deathbed blessing, to the wicked stepmother, to the wily old witch, Baba Yaga, to Vasilissa's adopted mother, even to the little doll—it is women who challenge Vasilissa to grow, who sustain her in her troubles, and who rejoice with her in her final triumph.

Elizabeth Winthrop
New York

Russian folklore is the expression of ancient concepts of the world in which forests, fields, rivers, and dwellings are imbued with enchantment and filled with supernatural characters—magic animals, swamp devils, mermaids, poltergeists, etc.

One such character is the old witch Baba Yaga. She appears in many tales and often plays a leading role. She always rides in a mortar, with a pestle and a broom, and lives in a hut on chicken legs. The hut can rotate on command; all one has to do is say, "Turn your face to me and your back to the forest."

Baba Yaga is usually very mean, but her role in Russian folklore varies—she is capable of good deeds as well as evil. I have dressed her in a *kitchka*—a cap with horns. When Russia adopted Christianity (in A.D. 988), the church fathers frowned on such caps, as they resembled the horns of the devil.

The costumes and setting in *Vasilissa the Beautiful* are roughly seventeenth-century. This period has become almost a tradition in illustrating Russian folktales.

Every Russian child knows and loves the tale of Vasilissa the Beautiful. I hope I have succeeded in capturing the atmosphere and flavor of the tale, and that American children will love it too.

Alexander Koshkin
Moscow

Elizabeth Winthrop

is the author of over thirty books for children of all ages, including THE CASTLE IN THE ATTIC (Holiday House), which won state awards in Vermont and California; A CHILD IS BORN: THE CHRISTMAS STORY and HE IS RISEN: THE EASTER STORY, both illustrated by Charles Mikolaycak (Holiday House); SHOES, illustrated by William Joyce; and, most recently, SLEDDING, illustrated by Sarah Wilson. Ms. Winthrop lives in New York City.

Alexander Koshkin

is renowned for his illustrations throughout Russia and Europe. His many books include a two-volume set of Grimm's fairy tales, published by Happy Books in Italy, and Rudyard Kipling's THE JUNGLE BOOK, published by Annaya in Spain. He has also illustrated many books published in Russia, including ALADDIN AND THE MAGIC LAMP and GOLDEN KEY: THE ADVENTURES OF BURATINO, a Russian Pinocchio story that won the bronze medal at the International Children's Book Contest in Leipzig in 1981.

Mr. Koshkin lives in Moscow, where he attended the Surikov Art College. When he is not drawing and painting, he restores eighteenth-and nineteenth-century furniture and collects model trains and ships.